3 —

SHA   S   D1550746

Th   of
kn

$22.95   50546020568375

DATE			

THE COMPANY OF KNAVES

THE COMPANY OF KNAVES

Simon Shaw

If any ask for me at court, report
You have left me in the company of knaves.

JOHN WEBSTER, *The White Devil*, IV, i.

St. Martin's Press   New York

A THOMAS DUNNE BOOK.
An imprint of St. Martin's Press.

Library of Congress Cataloging-in-Publication Data

Shaw, Simon.
    The company of knaves / Simon Shaw.
        p.   cm.
    "A Thomas Dunne book."
    ISBN 0-312-18069-1
    1. Fletcher, Philip (Fictitious character)—
Fiction.   I. Title.
PR6069.H3948C66   1998
823'.914—dc21   97-40345
                                        CIP

First published in Great Britain by HarperCollins
Publishers

First U.S. Edition: January 1998

10   9   8   7   6   5   4   3   2   1

To Susanna

Dedication

To my children, who I love enough to want to be healthy and whole for. To my editor Eric Vollen for being gentle with this first time author, and to my "SCCC Crew." Thanks for buying into being healthy enough to enjoy your vices.

Contents

Foreword

For anyone who has contemplated making a meaningful change in their life, you know that behavior change, and in particular weight loss, doesn't happen easily. In book 1 of *100 Small Steps,* my friend Mr. Keith "Temple" Trotter invites the reader to join him as he breaks down his weight loss experience into digestible bites.

Keith and I were introduced to one another during my work as a medical director at a regional health plan where he was also employed. At the time, I was piloting an effort at our mutual employer in partnership with Activ8 Mobile to address health through a holistic mind-body-spirit approach addressing awareness, choice, and accountability in our daily life. The day we met, Keith shared his story of *100 Small Steps* with me over lunch. He spoke of how he had figured out a way to address his own habits that were unhealthy and was well on his way to his current weight and healthier life. What he shared with me that day was nothing short of inspirational.

Throughout my 16-year career as a family physician I have been struck by how difficult it can be for individuals to change habits for the benefit of their health. Early on as a young physician, day after day, I would tell my patients with diabetes, obesity, and many other risk factors to change their lifestyle if they wished to avoid significant health problems down the road. As my practice evolved it became more and more apparent, not surprisingly in hindsight, that my approach was not overly successful. I had focused on managing chronic disease with appropriate prescription therapy yet wanted so badly to help through lifestyle intervention and removing physical barriers to activity. My own journey of learning how to support my patients in their lifestyle choices was humbling as I discovered how little I knew about making these difficult changes.

Since that time, I have walked alongside and supported many individuals in their efforts to change daily eating and activity habits as well as those who have successfully improved their health through weight loss, improved fitness, lowered blood pressure, and improved cholesterol results. While their personal gain—physically, emotionally, and financially—is important, the impact they are having on those around them, their children, and our healthcare system is not trivial. Poor behaviors in areas such as nutrition, physical activity, stress management, and tobacco use are contributing to chronic illnesses and unsustainable expenses in our healthcare system. These expenses ultimately are paid by you through higher health insurance premiums needed to cover the rising costs of caring for the population.

In the United States today, according to the Centers for Disease Control (CDC) 2009-10 data, 35.7 percent of adults were obese and 16.9 percent of children were obese. In addition, $149 billion spent on healthcare in 2008 were directly related to obesity. The average obese adult spent $1,429 dollars more on healthcare than their normal weight counterparts. The CDC reports:

- More than one-third of all adults do not meet recommendations for aerobic physical activity based on the 2008 Physical Activity Guidelines for Americans, and 23 percent report no leisure-time physical activity at all in the preceding month.
- In 2007, less than 22 percent of high school students and only 24 percent of adults reported eating five or more servings of fruits and vegetables per day.[1]

Many organizations currently are addressing and will continue to address population health by providing opportunities for you to improve your own health habits through policy changes, employer sponsored wellness programs and incentives, physician or provider-led services, among others. In spite of these efforts, finding your individual desire to make sustainable changes in your own life based on what is important to you will be more effective than any organizations efforts.

This is why *100 Small Steps* is so important. The authentic nature of how Keith shared his experiences with me at lunch was inspiring and thought-provoking and shows up powerfully in this text. His approach is practical and shows how several simple, achievable actions lead to a significant impact on one's health. Most important, he shares his "aha" moment that allowed him to get past his own self defenses that were "protecting" him from seeing his own state of health. Do you know of someone else who had their "aha" moment? Have you missed yours or intentionally avoided it like Keith did for so long?

Trotter focuses on some common themes through the book; "food is fuel" and should not be confused with something to sooth emotional distress, needing to be honest with oneself and identify where you are creating self-protective barriers to self-honesty. He shares real examples that are raw and authentic in discussing the role of social support and addressing mental health.

Those who are successful tend to have a few things in common: achieving awareness of their own condition or state, setting a clear goal, and choosing small sustainable steps that continue to move them towards achieving that goal.

As a result, I am excited and honored to be writing the foreword to Trotter's book. Throughout my healthcare career I've seen the need as well as the difficulty in enacting behavior change: one on one during patient care, working at a health plan with a focus on employer health, and now with a large retail health care provider. My own career path has led me closer to where individuals make their daily decisions, where they buy their groceries, fitness equipment and apparel, prescription medication, as well as over-the-counter products for self-care.

While I hope to be able to provide better opportunities for individuals to engage in healthier behaviors, Trotter provides a reminder there is not an easy path or quick fix. There will continue to be convenient excuses available every day, and you can choose to shape the reality around you to be detrimental to or supportive of your own health. While you read *100 Small Steps,* choose to identify and address your own habits that are limiting your short- and long-term health. Make your plan public, engage your support network, family, friends, and coworkers in holding you accountable.

—**Kevin Ronneberg**, MD,
Medical Director, Target Corporation

Acknowledgments

I would like to take a moment to personally thank and acknowledge the following people and organizations for their involvement in my life and contributions to the health and wellness of the communities and people they serve. The information, knowledge, and inspirations they provided were key factors leading towards my enlightenment and success. Thank you, and please keep up the good work that you are doing.

Carrie Riggin: www.triangle.com
Jim Benson: www.personalkanban.com
Paul Gillard, PhD Transformation Assoc., Inc.
Rachel Radwinski, PhD, Transformation Assoc., Inc.
Mike "2 Meal Mike" O'Donnell
Dr. Kevin Ronneberg
Dave Dickey, Second Story Sales
Pat Sukhum
Tammy Strome Cre8tion Fitness & Wellness

Dr. James Beckerman, www.lifescript.com
Dr. Lisa Rankin, Owning Pink Center
Tony Schober, www.coachcalorie.com
Chrissy Wallace, Crossfit Duvall
www.ririanproject.com
www.serenejourney.com
Bershan Shaw, www.URAWarrior.com
Chenoa Maxwell www.chenoamaxwell.com

Introduction

Congratulations on taking the first steps towards becoming a healthier and more beautiful you! Throughout these pages, you'll see, just as I have, that this odyssey of transformation is about changing your mindset first, which will then transform your body. The journey starts with a few simple questions and ends with execution. Ask yourself, "Why am I doing this?" "Am I really committed to the difficult changes ahead that are necessary to have the life and body I desire?" Friends, I have to tell you, this is a critical crossroad, and these questions deserve serious consideration. This isn't about choosing the health and wellness "cause célèbre" off some blog and pinning it to your chest. What I'm asking you to do is engage in deep contemplation about some real and—hopefully—transformative motivations that have led you to believe why—after all the time, energy, effort, and money you've spent on dieting and gym memberships—that this time, things are going to be different. This time, I'm going to make changes to my life—for life.

It might seem counterintuitive that thinking and not doing would be the first step in the process, and I agree. But rest assured, I wouldn't have lost over 160 pounds—and kept it off—had I not engaged in these beliefs. About halfway through the process I came to the realization that I had to muddle through and then sweep away all of the physiological programming, coping mechanisms, and marketing hype before truly getting to the heart of the matter. I began to realize that I had to "buy into" and recreate the symbiotic relationships between my head, body, and heart so that the motivations were existent and belonged to me distinctively. Once this process was complete, I was able to answer for myself the timeless question of unstoppable force and immovable object. In my case, if the unstoppable force is the will to live a healthy, fulfilled, and productive life, and the immovable object is morbid obesity, then obesity had to get the hell out of the way!

This part of the process is yours, and I cannot—scratch that—*will* not be able to tell you how to get it done, for it's an intimate process deserving of as much time, care, devotion, and attention as you would give your lover. I chose to crystallize my motivations by writing them down and then posting them in as many visible places as possible. I kept them in close reach and in full view first thing in the morning and at bedtime. I made sure that I also shared those motivations with my dearest friends and loved ones so that they could act as my external will, when my internal will just wasn't enough to get it done.

A final note—and this part is for your friends and loved ones, so please allow them to read it. Stop being an enabler. Sometimes when you truly love someone, it's in their best interest for you to hurt their feelings. Tough love, right? As an adult male, I was afflicted with what I call the "I was buff in high school, so I must be buff now" disorder. I had no idea that I looked more like the Michelin Tire Man, and I was pissed when I found out. I felt betrayed and the brunt of some longstanding running joke. I was morbidly obese and everyone knew it, except me. I just wish someone had the strength to tell me. Don't be that person. Talk openly and candidly about your concerns for their health. Show you care with your support and your strength. Trust me: they'll love you for it, and you might just save someone's life. Tough love is still love.

BOOK 1

You Gotta Think Right!

In my attempt to find the real me underneath the layers of my dysfunctional coping mechanisms, I discovered there's an almost symbiotic relationship between depression and obesity. In March 2010 in the *Archives of General Psychiatry* a meta-analysis of seventeen community-based cross-sectional studies among adults revealed a "positive overall association between depression and obesity."[1] What follows in the study are more highfalutin words and explanations of how you can trust the numbers than you can shake a stick at, but the overall gist is what we have known all along. Your mind and body are connected, and if the mind isn't healthy the body won't be, and vice-versa. Now, you would think that this information would be readily available to the public at large, and in the interest of public health, the media, the medical community, and your grandmother would be taking up the cause. I mean, obesity in America is only at epidemic proportions, right? Fifty-eight million of us are overweight (19 percent), forty million obese (13 percent), and three million are morbidly obese (1 percent).[2] What does this mean? It means that more than a third of our population has a 55 percent increased risk of developing depression, and those who do develop depression have a 58 percent increased risk of becoming overweight over time. Let's see if you can recognize the pattern in my own personal journal notes.

December 4, 2000

"I have said this to myself at least 100 times and I have decided to say it for the last time ever in my life. This is the absolute last year that I will be overweight and out of shape! I am 29 years old and I weigh 308 pounds. I am six feet tall and I am dying. I'm dying physically, spiritually, and emotionally, and it's all because I hate who I am."

You Gotta Think Right
January 1, 2002

"I am determined to do a couple of things this year. (1) I am going to build my best body ever. I have let myself go and I know good and full well that it is going to take more than 12 weeks to get there but you have to start somewhere and I figure a twelve-week program is as good a place as any. So I have decided to make this new chapter in my life the plot and subplot. The main story line here is that after all these years of neglect and medical problems (diabetes, pernicious anemia, lupus anticoagulant, asthma, etc.) I am going to get back in shape and be sexy again so that I can (2) take the world of opera by storm!"

June 5, 2002

"It has been almost a week since I started my new training program. I hadn't been able to feel my feet for a while and now I can feel them just fine and I don't have that nagging tingling or numb sensation anymore. That is a hell of an accomplishment for a 300-plus-pound man with diabetes, lupus, and a B12 deficiency."

My journals go on like that for years, chronicling my health issues, unhappiness with my weight, and depression over my abusive childhood. It is a vicious, painful cycle like the one that has crippled an entire nation. Yet the only solutions apparently available to us are in pharmaceutical, pseudo-pharmaceutical, surgical and sweat-and-starve forms. You've seen the infomercials. Someone with a hot body shows up on TV while you're sitting there at 2 a.m. licking the last half-hour's cheesy-poof dust off your fingers and cramming a home-made mayonnaise, fried-egg, Swiss and cheddar-cheese hoagie down your gullet. You see his rippling muscles, hear his sob story about how just four short months ago he looked just like you, but now, thanks to the break-through ingredients in Belly Be Gone!, he dropped five pants sizes and is now dating Kobe Bryant's second cousin twice removed. That's when you notice your chest is getting tight and your body's sore from just the thought of spending the next ninety days popping pills and treating your body like a slave. This portion of the battle is psychological and you cannot win it without first fighting it head-on and winning it decisively. So the first thing you have to do is…

Know *Why* You Are Doing It!

"He who has a why to live for can bear almost any how."
—Friedrich Nietzsche

What the Experts Say

The *why* is more important than the *how*. The *why* makes it personal and affords you the opportunity to buy into, internalize, and become intimate with what you have to accomplish. The *how* is sterile and foreign, and it dredges up all of your worst fears about Big Brother and the boogeyman actualized in HD. The *how* is given to you. The *why* comes from within you. The *how* can be all wrong for you, but the *why* is your baby, and in order to have a beautiful, healthy, strong baby you have to nurture and promote her well-being.

How I Did It

I posted my reasons all over the house. The main "reason" was a photo that showed up on my Facebook time line of how absolutely grotesque I looked at the New Year's Eve party. I made sure my reasons were in close reach whenever I went to the bathroom or the kitchen, watched television, got ready to ride my bike, whenever and wherever there was an opportunity for me to lose the psychological war by rationalizing or negotiating what I called "the lesser path" (You know: the path that doesn't hurt as much or demand as much from you). I just kept looking, and I keep looking, at that damned picture of myself at almost four-hundred pounds, spilling out of that wicker chair with a plate of food balanced on my stomach (why is it always a plate of food?) and I found the strength to pull those laces a little tighter and get out there and make this thing happen. I thought about all the times my little girls wanted to be active with their father and the excuses I was constantly giving them as to why I couldn't be. Would I one day be too fat, disabled, and tired to walk my beautiful daughters down the aisle? I wrote my motivations down and looked at that god-awful picture first thing in the morning, and they were the last things I saw and dreamed about at night. And yes, I did exercise in my dreams.

Step 1 Question

Why Am I Doing This?

Remove the Words "Diet," "Low fat," and "Low Calorie" from Your Kitchen and Vocabulary

"Food is fuel—no more, no less."
—Temple

What the Experts Say

Your mind-set influences your taste and choice in food. A study published in July 2011 by the National Center for Biotechnology Information shows that foods labeled "diet," "reduced fat," "low fat," or "low calorie" can actually lead you to consume more (approximately 25 percent more).[1] When the levels of energy in the body become low your stomach produces a peptide called ghrelin which signals hunger pangs in the brain. When food is consumed, the levels of ghrelin in the body decrease, producing the sense of satiation. The study was simple. Forty-six participants were asked to enjoy two sessions, a week apart, of free milk-shake tasting. The only catch was that they had to read and rate the label as well as the taste of the milk shake. The participants were led to believe that they had received two different milk shakes, but in reality the only difference was the label. Long story short, the milk shake labeled "low calorie" did not reduce the required levels of ghrelin in order for the subjects to feel psychologically satisfied. "In such cases, people tend to consume more food and are hence at risk of developing obesity."[2]

How I Did It

No, I did not throw away all the food labeled in this way. I just made sure that I treated all food exactly the same way. Food is fuel—no more and no less. It's not a reward and you don't "deserve" to be able to pig out because you [enter random reason here]. This was a huge struggle for me because, like most of us, I had fostered and embraced an unhealthy relationship with food and had fallen for the marketing like a cheerleader goes for starting quarterbacks. I wanted to be able to eat until I was full and be assured that it was ok because I was consuming fewer calories when exactly the opposite was true. One of the tricks of the trade is to replace the fat in low-fat foods with sugar. So the amount of fat is truly reduced but the carbohydrates have increased and can actually lead to food having higher caloric values than the foods not labeled "low fat." Moral of the story for me?

- Food is fuel—no more, no less.
- Be present in your choices.
- Marketers are not your friends.
- Relationships are with people, not with food.

Step 2 Question

How Much of the Food in Your House Has This Labeling?

Be Present in Every Choice

"I attribute my success to this:
I never gave or took an excuse"
—Florence Nightingale

What the Experts Say

In 2006 food companies spent $1.6 billion just to market mostly soda, fast-food, and cereal to children. In that same year quick service restaurants sold over 1.2 billion kids meals with toys. Now, you may be asking yourself why that pertains to you? Well, if you're a Gen Xer you already know the answer. We watch a lot of TV programming that would be part of the target market. According to the Center for a New American Dream, brand loyalty can be established as early as age two! This is loyalty that lasts a lifetime. The

Kellogg Foundation discovered that Americans create an emotional link to food companies as nurturers early in their lives. Thus, thinking critically about food companies "can violate people's deep desire to be secure."[1] Sound familiar? Emotional links? Sense of security? Remember how I had created an unhealthy relationship with food? Well I guess I had some help.

How I Did It

Food is fuel, food is fuel, food is fuel. No more and no less. I told myself this whenever I went to pay for gas or buy groceries (which is why I never went grocery shopping hungry), or when I went to the movies, or anyplace where I knew I would be interacting casually with food (Sitting down for a meal took a different mindset). This included watching TV with the kids and noticing how the billion dollar marketing machines vie for their loyalty, which then manifests itself in the constant nagging of their parents to buy this and that. There's a reason junk food is at a kid's eye level in stores. How many times have you had to bend over to grab your favorite candy bar? Do you even know? Or has it just become habit? This one is still tough for me today. Between the demands of work, kids, spouses, partners, and social networks, life is more stressful than ever. Sometimes all you want to do is turn off and go into autopilot. Guess what? Marketers have spent billions of dollars to discover that's exactly what they want you to do—which is why stores are set up the way they are. You unconsciously reach for and purchase whatever is closest and easiest. So since I live in a small town and know the gas station owner, I asked very nicely that she put a bowl of fruit out so that I could buy that when I came into her shop. And it worked. Almost three years later the bowl is still there and I have yet to see any rotten fruit in it.

Step 3 Questions

Are You Aware?

1. What is your favorite food?
2. When did you first realize this?
3. At what age was it introduced to you?
4. Would you let your loved ones
   eat it as much as you do?

Be Brutally Honest with Yourself about Yourself

"Ruthlessly compete with your own best self."
—Apollo 13 Engineers

This one is mainly for the "men folks," as my grandmother would say. In the book *Men are from Mars, Women Are from Venus* we were introduced to the concept that, in general, women and men view themselves in perceptively different ways. Women are über-critical and men are... well, we're just men. I looked like a swollen tick, but in my mind, and when I looked in the mirror, I was God's gift to the opposite sex. It was really pathetic. And worse, I was putting my friends in the unenviable position of humoring me and watching me die a not-so-slow death, or telling me flat out that I looked like my man Blob from Gigglesnort

Hotel. (They had chosen the former btw.) The second-worst day of my life was seeing that tagged Facebook picture of me (all 386 pounds of me) sitting in a wicker chair with a plate of food, no lap, no neck, sporting a D Cup, and more chins than Dexter Jettster from Star Wars. The spell was broken. I could no longer mentally control the message and it was devastating. I had to face the fact that I was morbidly obese. I had created an environment that fostered my obesity, and was willfully turning a blind eye to how unhealthy and unattractive I had become because of it. I cried, got really pissed off at my wife and friends, then quickly apologized and fixed blame where it belonged, and that was with me. I'd noticed that there were no pictures of me around the house. No vacations, no pics with my buddies, nothing. I quickly realized that this was all done on purpose. I had to look at myself in the mirror, but I didn't have to look at pictures of my obesity. Subconsciously I didn't like how I looked, so I wouldn't look unless I could control the message. I couldn't control the message of someone else's eye, but I could my own. So from that day forward, I took pictures. Lots and lots of pictures. I celebrated the victories when they looked good and I got a good cry when old Stay Puft (*Ghostbusters,* c. 1984) looked back and, waving, said "Hey! Remember me?" Till this day, though I've lost 160 pounds, I stay brutally honest with myself. I am still overweight. I have a body mass index (BMI) of 32.3, down from 52.4, which made me morbidly obese. My goal weight of 220 would give me a BMI of exactly 30 and I would still be classified as overweight (At six feet, zero inches, my ideal weight is less than or equal to 184 pounds). I will never get too far below 220—my bones and organs weigh more than that—but the numbers are a great way for me to track how I'm doing. They keep me honest, and that is restoring quality to my life.

Body Mass Index (BMI) Table
(Adult Men & Women)

	Underweight			Normal						Overweight					Obese					
BMI	16	17	18	19	20	21	22	23	24	25	26	27	28	29	30	31	32	33	34	35
Height							Body Weight (pounds)													
4'10"	77	82	86	91	96	100	105	110	115	119	124	129	134	138	143	148	153	158	162	167
4'11"	79	84	89	94	99	104	109	114	119	124	128	133	138	143	148	153	158	163	168	173
5'	82	87	92	97	102	107	112	118	123	128	133	138	143	148	153	158	163	168	174	179
5'1"	85	90	96	100	106	111	116	122	127	132	137	143	148	153	158	164	169	174	180	185
5'2"	88	93	99	104	109	115	120	126	131	136	142	147	153	158	164	169	175	180	186	191
5'3"	91	96	102	107	113	118	124	130	135	141	146	152	158	163	169	175	180	186	191	197
5'4"	93	99	105	110	116	122	128	134	140	145	151	157	163	169	174	180	186	192	197	204
5'5"	96	102	108	114	120	126	132	138	144	150	156	162	168	174	180	186	192	198	204	210
5'6"	99	106	112	118	124	130	136	142	148	155	161	167	173	179	186	192	198	204	210	216
5'7"	102	109	115	121	127	134	140	146	153	159	166	172	178	185	191	198	204	211	217	223
5'8"	105	112	118	125	131	138	144	151	158	164	171	177	184	190	197	203	210	216	223	230
5'9"	109	115	122	128	135	142	149	155	162	169	176	182	189	196	203	209	216	223	230	236
5'10"	112	119	126	132	139	146	153	160	167	174	181	188	195	202	209	216	222	229	236	243
5'11"	115	122	129	136	143	150	157	165	172	179	186	193	200	208	215	222	229	236	243	250
6'	118	125	133	140	147	154	162	169	177	184	191	199	206	213	221	228	235	242	250	258
6'1"	121	129	137	144	151	159	166	174	182	189	197	204	212	219	227	235	242	250	257	265
6'2"	125	133	140	148	155	163	171	179	186	194	202	210	218	225	233	241	249	256	264	272
6'3"	128	136	144	152	160	168	176	184	192	200	208	216	224	232	240	248	256	264	272	279

Source: Adapted from Clinical Guidelines on the Identification, Evaluation, and Treatment of Overweight and Obesity in Adults, 1998.

Step 4 Questions

Honesty Check

"What's it going to be—reasons or results?"
—Art Turock

1. When you look in the mirror, what do you see?
2. Are there pictures of you in the house where people can see them?

Focus on the Whole Life

*"You can't make footprints in the sands of time
if you're sitting on your butt. And who wants to
make buttprints in the sands of time?"*
—Bob Moawad

At the end of the day weight loss can be achieved only by placing an emphasis on physical and mental health and nutrition. You can obsess over counting calories, half starving yourself, and doing Lord-knows-what unhealthy exercise routine, for only so long. Willpower is finite and, unfortunately for you, it's not strong enough to fight millennia of physiological programming that says, "Pack it in, my friend. You're not safe, and you don't know when the next time we're gonna eat is." (Trust me: it's worse when you've known utter poverty firsthand, like I have.) This is one of the main reasons diets just don't work. They focus on one aspect of the problem instead of taking a holistic approach. First, you have to deal with the psychological reasons why we (especially Americans) have developed unhealthy relationships with food. Don't be fooled: you need a professional counselor for this part. It won't work long term without one. It wasn't a diet that helped me; it was the desire to make sustained, living, breathing, transformative life changes that took off over a third (41 percent) of my overall body weight with no plans to see it ever return!

Be Ye Not
Afraid to Fail!

"I am not concerned that you have fallen:
I am concerned that you arise."
—Abraham Lincoln

Look, there was just no way that I was going to go right into some program where at almost four-hundred pounds there were going to be ninety straight days of increasingly intense and insane levels of physical exertion when I had just spent the previous ninety days on the couch blowing 40 to 50 bucks a week on the finest grade cheesy poofs, beer, cheap cheese and lunchmeat, and soft white bread. It was going to take time and there were going to be a lot of false starts along the way. It hurt like hell; I'm not going to lie. I hated it. I hated feeling and being weak. I wanted to be able to wake up one morning over the hump, and run a mile without feeling like my legs were on fire and my lungs about to burst. Guess what? That day never came. I still hate running, but I beat it. It kept slapping me around, knocking me down and calling me names when I cried, but I just closed my eyes, put my head down and kept swinging. And like any bully, after a few hard licks on the chin, all of a sudden he had to back off a brotha and go find someone else to pick on. I failed a lot, and when I think about it I want to beat myself up, but the journey taught me not to be so afraid of failure.

I had a girlfriend once that used to say all the time that mental illness is mostly a direct result of the avoidance of pain. I didn't know what she meant then but I think I know now. We build all of our coping mechanisms around the avoidance of pain in all of its forms, but mostly around shame. We use that dysfunction to build the walls that we think protect us from pain but serve ultimately only to limit our true abilities. Take that away and you unleash the power of true human potential. Who can stop an individual who's not afraid to get knocked down and just keeps standing, lacing them up a little tighter each time? No bully I know. Go get 'em!

Step 6 Questions

The Sum of Your Fears

1. What are you afraid of?
2. Are these fears reasonable?
3. What would you accomplish if you weren't so afraid?

See a Licensed Counselor

"There is nothing either good or bad,
but thinking makes it so."
—William Shakespeare

I cannot stress this enough. If you are anything like me, your walls of dysfunction make Jericho look like the first house in the story of the three little pigs. I've always been a big boy. I'd been called "fat" for so long that I used to berate people "playing the dozens"[1] as simple and unimaginative whenever they said the words. (Seriously, a veritable plethora of issues you could snap[2] on me about and the best you could come up with is "Hey, you're fat"?) In fact, I was never fat as a child, but I stood a whole head above my peers for years and had a build that was suited better for plowing fields than for playing tennis. But the constant barrage had an effect on me over time. It hurt my feelings, so I built my own ways to cope with it which included being as mean and nasty to people about it as I possibly could when it came up. According to the criteria laid out in the *Diagnostic and Statistical Manual of Mental Disorders*, fourth edition (DSM-IV), approximately one in every five adults (22.1 percent) suffers from a diagnosable mental disorder in a given year.[3] Be it from bullying or abusive home lives, either way, that equates to approximately sixty-six million individuals. When it comes to depression, the numbers are staggering. Of the 22 percent of individuals that can be diagnosed with a mental disorder, 10 percent are depressive disorders that affect twice as many women as men. Four out of the ten leading causes of disability in America—unipolar major depression (1), bipolar disorder (6), schizophrenia (9), and obsessive compulsive disorder (10)—are mental disorders.[4] The deck is stacked against us, but due to social stigmas ("What, are you crazy?" is what I heard...a lot.) we don't seek the professional help we need. A theme that will return time and again throughout this book is that a healthy body follows a healthy mind. If you won't do it for yourself, do it for someone that loves you and wants to see you healthy, whole, and happy.

Step 7 Questions

Discussion Time

1. Have you spoken with a licensed counselor?
2. What would you like to discuss?
3. If not, what's holding you back?
4. Is it reasonable that it *would* hold you back?

Understand Feast vs. Famine in the Brain

"Cuz I don't know when we will have it again."
—Collin Trotter

What the Experts Say

Today almost seven billion people live on planet earth and a full 15 percent of us could audition for the lead role in *Big Momma's House* without a fat suit. In 1962 Dr. James Neel, an American geneticist posited that if we looked at the habits of our foraging ancestors and the feast-or-famine conditions they faced, we would find a possible explanation. Neel suggested that since food was in scarce supply, the body had adopted what he called a "thrifty metabolism" which, in effect, trained itself to store excess dietary energy as fat when food was in abundant supply. This nifty trick would have afforded us a survival advantage during periods of prolonged shortage. Fast forward several thousand years, when food (at least for the industrialized world) is in abundant supply, and our foraging-adapted genes would now be rendered obsolete or, as he put it, "detrimental by progress."[1] In other words, the caloric needs of someone eating a meal after hunting and foraging for days, as opposed to shopping for it at the local Piggly Wiggly,[2] are demonstrably different. Yet our genes are constantly screaming at us to pack it in because, in their world, Piggly Wiggly cannot be trusted as a stable and reliable source of sustenance. If you have children, especially teenage boys, you see it play out in front of you every day. My boys can empty out a kitchen cabinet with more ferocity and wonton abandon than twice the number of biblical plagues. I once asked my son why he felt that it was his God-given right to eat a whole box of cereal, and he told me flat out, "Cuz I don't know when we will have it again." It's not only our genes that are working against us, but the way we think about food. We are worried about food in the richest countries in the world and our bodies are co-signing that agreement with impunity.

How I Did It

This was really hard. I come from a large family of mostly boys, so when it came time to eat, if you were slow, or late, or just *happened* to fall down on the way to the table, more than likely you didn't eat. I had to actively train myself to reject the idea that if I didn't eat it now, it wouldn't be there for me later. Weird, huh? Without even realizing it, I had made a few, shall we say, agreements about the world I lived in and my relationship with food. I was in the top 25 percent of American wage earners but was subconsciously concerned about where my next meal was coming from? How does that happen? Blame the genes.

Step 8 Question

What Agreements Have You Made?

Know that "Willpower" Is Finite!

"Spectacular achievement is always
preceded by spectacular preparation."
—Dr. Robert Schuller

What the Experts Say

The last decade of research has spawned two schools of thought on the subject. Today I'm here to introduce you to the term Decision Fatigue[1] which has recently entered into the lexicon of psychology. It is based on psychologist Roy F. Baumeister's homage to Freud's Energy Model of Self where the self or ego depended on mental activities involving the transfer of energy. In order to prove these theories Baumeister conducted a series of experiments at Case Western University and Florida State University.

These experiments demonstrated that there is a finite store of mental energy for decisioning, willpower, and self-control. As the subjects exercised self-control, they were less likely to fend off other temptations. So willpower, as it happens, turns out to be much more than just a folk concept or metaphor. It is in fact a mental energy that can be depleted through exertion.

How I Did It

This was one of those aha moments for me. My mom had seven kids, worked two jobs, and went to school full-time when I was a kid. So at 5 a.m. we had to be a highly trained, well-organized machine. We didn't have time to think about anything. We needed to be *doing* or there was hell to pay. We did everything the night before. We chose our clothes, made lunches, packed book bags, and took baths, all before bedtime (8 p.m. Monday through Sunday), so when that alarm went off we were officially on autopilot. This was a habit that was ingrained early and just evolved into my adult life. I'm a list maker, so naturally I made lists. At the end of the day I made a list of all the decisions that needed to be made for the next day. Living a fuller, more engaged, and healthier life was one of the decisions that I needed pounded into my psyche and soul, so it went on the list and I made sure to acknowledge it in my reflective as well as my prospective decisioning processes. (Did I live up to the decisions I made and how will I live up to them tomorrow?) One of the reasons it worked for me was that since I felt in my heart that the decision to live and be healthy was already made and validated every night, and then again in the morning, there was no need to expend any additional energy on it. I was not depleting my stores of willpower or self-control. In fact, my resolve was stronger due to the fact that I just refused to make myself out to be a liar (which, by the way, was another of the many and varied reasons to catch a "beat down"[2] at 5266 S. State Street, Apt. 909, my old address in the inner city projects of Chicago). It seemed to me, at the time, to be a juvenile, even silly thing to do as an adult. I guess it's sometimes the small, silly things we do for our loved ones that count the most.

Step 9 Questions

What's Your Process?

1. How do you make decisions?
2. What's going on your list?

Minimize Stress

"Our bodies are constantly responding
in a fight-or-flight way."
—Temple

What the Experts Say

In a fairly recent study conducted by the Departments of Psychiatry and Biomedical Engineering at the University of Cincinnati College of Medicine it was discovered that chronic stress and the production of cortisol-induced insulin are main contributing factors that can lead to increases in body fat and obesity.[1]

Most people are aware of the behavioral and psychological factors concerning stress-related obesity. When you're stressed you have trouble maintaining a healthy lifestyle. It translates into eating often, even when you're not hungry, or eating high-calorie or fatty fast-foods, because you don't have time to prepare something healthy. And the *pièce de résistance* of it all is that you're too exhausted to exercise regularly due to the very same stress.

Here's how stress is supposed to work: when faced with a stressful situation, the body triggers the stress response, or what is commonly referred to as the fight-or-flight response. When that response is triggered, the body secretes cortisol, adrenaline, and other stress hormones, and blood pressure rises along with the breathing and heart rates. This increases the energy readily available to the body for action while non-fight-or-flight processes like digestion are decreased. This process is geared for short-term use and is self-regulating. When the stress is relieved, and cortisol and adrenaline levels decrease, the body is supposed to return to normal function. The problem is that in today's world the stress just keeps on coming. When stress is overwhelming, constant, and excessive, the fight-or-flight response never turns off. The resulting situation is a body constantly making adrenaline and cortisol. Adrenaline helps fat cells release energy so that the body is ready to use it. Cortisol stimulates fat and carbohydrate metabolism, which leads to increased glucose (blood sugar) levels and the release of insulin, making us hungry so that we feel the need to replace the energy we expended in our fight-or-flight response. Now, you will remember that in Step 8 I mentioned that the caloric needs of someone who hunted and foraged for days were demonstrably different from those of someone that shops for food at the local Piggly Wiggly. Well the same is true here. Our bodies are constantly responding in a fight-or-flight way, but the stresses are traffic jams, crying babies, crashing computers, unrealistic expectations at work and home, and the list goes on. The body's caloric needs for dealing appropriately with such activities are patently different from those of someone confronting a band of invaders or a saber-toothed tiger. The environment has changed, but the body's responses have not. So that extra cortisol running through your body triggers insulin production which in turn makes the body think that it needs to refuel, when in all actuality you haven't used the energy that has already been released to you. So what happens? Besides setting yourself up to become insulin resistant, which may lead to diabetes, you wind up converting the released energy and the newly consumed calories into fat, which makes you more susceptible to the disease.

How I Did It

Once I did this research it became clear that I needed to do two things. First, I needed to keep my system flushed out. It's the accumulation of these hormones that causes the problem, so I needed to stay active enough to be continuously burning the fuel and hydrated enough so the waste would pass from my body. And secondly, I needed to seek counseling so that I could learn the coping skills necessary to navigate successfully under today's über-stressful conditions. Learning that I cannot control every situation, and that every action is not a personal slight or affront, went a long way toward changing my thought patterns and eating habits so that I could lose the weight and keep it off.

Step 10 Questions

All Stressed Out?

1. What triggers your stress response?
2. Is it reasonable that these triggers cause you stress?
3. How do you cope with stress today?

Learn How to Meditate

"Your mind can focus on fear, worry,
problems, negativity or despair. Or it can
focus on confidence, opportunity, solutions,
optimism, and success. You Decide."
—Don Ward

What the Experts Say

In the introduction of this book I freely admitted that it seemed counterintuitive that thinking, and not doing, would be the first, most critical step in the process. After all, you can't burn one ounce of fat off your body sitting in one spot and trying to open your mind to the universe. Or can you? Dr. Deepak Chopra, distinguished author, teacher, and fellow of the American College of Physicians, has produced a program that blends ancient Vedanta philosophy with modern medicine to provide meditative solutions that meet a wide variety of needs. Although medical experts have not been able to pinpoint the results you will achieve through meditation, a growing number of practitioners believe that meditation does have some health benefits. Dr. Chopra teaches that "Meditation can bring healing to the body and give strength to the intentions."

How I Did It

I am an early riser and have found that regular meditation is a valuable ritual in my life. As you have doubtless noticed by now, I am also a firm believer that weight loss is more than just a series of physical activities and food deprivations with the stated goal of burning more calories than you take in (Even that process starts in the mind). This is always going to be merely a temporary fix. The focal point of my meditation was on my desire to eat healthier foods and feel full and satisfied with my choices, and to visualize myself losing weight and feeling stronger, healthier, and more focused. My ritual was to rise early and sit in a room by myself in a chair, with my hands flat on my thighs and with my eyes closed, purging my body of negative energy through a series of three deep breaths. Using Dr. Chopra's method, I said out loud to myself, "I am stronger today than yesterday, I am healthier today than yesterday, I am more determined today than yesterday." I then whispered the same words to myself to help me internalize them and make them even more personal. Then, keeping that same whispered tone, I just thought about those three things while visualizing myself working out, running, smiling, trying on new clothes, and the like. For the next ten-to-fifteen minutes I allowed no negative thoughts, sounds, or visions to enter my world of peace and victory. The benefits to me were amazing and they made their way into all aspects of my personal and professional life. Now, meditation is a powerful mechanism that can prepare your mind and body for weight loss by changing your thinking and feelings surrounding the issue of weight loss, but you must still do the work of putting your vision into action. Daily meditation allows you to re-program your brain and to reduce stress. It also increases your mindfulness and brain function throughout the day, defending you against poor choices by reducing decision fatigue. I am willing to guarantee that by using these techniques your mission will get easier and be more fulfilling.

Know Your Numbers

"Ninety percent of obesity is preventable."
—Safeway Study (c. 2005)

What the Experts Say

In 2005 Safeway, the grocery-store chain, initiated a policy of rewarding its employees for engaging in healthy behavior. Their plan was based on several insights: (1) 70 percent of all health-care costs are the direct result of behavior; (2) 74 percent of all costs are confined to four chronic conditions (cardiovascular disease, cancer, diabetes and obesity); (3) 80 percent of cardiovascular disease and diabetes is preventable; (4) 60 percent of cancers are preventable; and (5) more than 90 percent of obesity is preventable. Yep, that's right, over 90 percent! Safeway was able to build a culture of health and fitness in four years, keeping per capita health expense flat, while the rest of the country saw increases of up to 38 percent[1] over the same time period. How, you ask? By biometric screening: four simple tests that took less than ten minutes and a mechanism to track changes in the results. According to Safeway's results, if the country had adopted their initiatives in 2005, our nation's healthcare bill would have been $550 billion lower in 2009 and we would have been a much healthier and aware workforce.

How I Did It

It helped that I was the controller for one of the nation's hottest startups whose purpose it was to introduce these measures to the workforce. In 2007 RedBrick Health (RBH) was created with the express goal of engaging employees to help rein in the cost of employer-sponsored health insurance. I had my first biometric screening and was shocked. Being a Lean Six Sigma practitioner, I knew one thing was universally true: things that get measured get done. If you're tracking it, you're generally going to do something about it when it goes south. Four simple tests were all I needed to get a good baseline of my health goals, and it was off to the races. I got my numbers for diabetes risk (glucose A1C), high blood pressure, cholesterol (LDL and HDL), and obesity through a Body Mass Index. Now, there is a lot of controversy surrounding body types and BMI, but even if you don't subscribe to BMI measurement as a whole, it is still a great way to compare yourself to the populace and assess your risk factors for obesity. RBH also has a tool that allows you to track your numbers over time, along with your physical activity, calories burned, caloric intake, and progress toward your stated goals. It was tedious, at first, to record and remember to enter the information, but once I made it a ritual it became easy peasy. If you have a health plan that offers biometric screening, take advantage of it. If not, talk to your doctor about it and get the ball rolling towards a better you.

Step 12 Questions

Know Thyself!

"Things that get measured get done."
—Temple

What is your:

- Height
- Weight
- BMI
- Cholesterol LDL/HDL
- Blood pressure
- A1C (fasting)
- Blood glucose (average daily)
- Are they in the normal range?

Food and Emotions Don't Mix

*"Seventy-five percent of overeating
is caused by emotions."*
—**"Emotional Eating and Weight Loss"**

What the Experts Say

According to nutritional experts, seventy-five percent of overeating is caused by emotions.[1] People often eat to relieve stress or to get something off their minds. The kicker is that stress, and the insulin jump that goes with it, may actually cause you to crave high-sugar, high-carbohydrate foods —foods that go straight to your waistline and cause you even more stress. At worst, it can take over your life and cause you to eat uncontrollably for extended periods of time.

How I Did It

I have trigger foods, but unlike Step 2, where I kept the food around and was just careful in the way I consumed it, I actually did remove them from the cabinets. (Remember the cheesy poofs!) I also had to find other things to do besides eat when I was stressed, upset, depressed, or otherwise having a difficult time maintaining "presence." I developed habits and rituals to try and control those emotional episodes, keep stress low, and my sanity intact. When I felt something coming on I would use the breathing technique we discussed in Step 11 (Learn How to Meditate), then I would do one, or sometimes all, of the following:

- Go for a walk or jog.
- Look at that damned picture again.
- Talk to somebody, anybody, and let them know I was struggling.
- Journal, or just read old posts in my journal.
- Put the bad stuff in a teacup for portion control (damned cheesy poofs).
- Eat veggies or applesauce or anything with high nutritional value in a smaller serving size by using a small plate or cup.

I wasn't always successful and I had setbacks, but I gave as good as I got from my body and emotions, and in the end I had a new body and a new outlook on life.

Step 13 Question

Will Work for Cheesy Poofs

What are my trigger foods?

Surround Yourself with the Positive

"When building a team, I always search first for people who love to win. If I can't find any of those, I look for people who hate to lose."
—Ross Perot

What the Experts Say

Carrie Riggin, a columnist over at www.Triangle.com, says it succinctly and best: "Get rid of toxic people. *Period!*" (I've added the emphasis.) Riggin goes on to say that we all know deep down that the person we used to be won't be good enough to transform us into the victorious individual of tomorrow. This also applies to the happy-hour crowd, the weekend-booze and barbecue crowd currently using your couch to sleep it off. No one is saying that these good friends have <u>no</u> place in your life, but if they can't or won't convert with you to a new, healthier, and more responsible lifestyle, then unfortunately they should occupy a diminished place in your life. Incorporating the people worth keeping around, along with your new healthy passions, is a critically important factor toward maintaining your long-term physical and mental health.

How I Did It

Like Ms. Riggin, I lost some friends. Guys who were with me through some pretty difficult and embarrassing times, but ultimately were not good for me and what I was trying to do.

The good thing is that most of the crew I hung out with were very supportive, and collectively we lost almost four-hundred pounds together. There were some difficult conversations, and days when I felt like an awful traitor who had turned his back on someone that really needed him. But at the end of the day, my desire to be healthy for my babies trumped all. They needed me more than my drinking buddies did. They were there, along with my positive support system, when I needed to tell someone how I was struggling. They told me I could do it. And better yet, they told me how they were going to do it with me. They offered encouragement and support when I needed it, and they told me to stop crying like a baby when I needed that too. I love my support system. Seek out yours and you will too.

Step 14 Questions

Happy People

"Get rid of toxic people. Period!"
—**Carrie Riggin**

1. Who are the people in my support system?
2. Will they help me become the victorious individual of tomorrow?

Celebrate Small Victories

*"Celebrate incremental victories! Take credit for jobs
well done, and do them even better next time."*
—Jim Benson

What the Experts Say

Jim Benson, co-author of Personal Kanban, an online tool
to visualize, organize and complete work, says it this way:
"Life is short. Crap is Plentiful. Thus defines the human
condition." Jim is a collaborative management consultant,
and since I'm a guy that studies and employs Lean Six
Sigma and Agile Project Management techniques, I just
eat this stuff up. Jim writes that there are three ways that
projects get into trouble. First: Having a rigid definition
of success which in turn almost inevitably creates a self-
fulfilling prophecy that guarantees failure in the attempt
to avoid failure. Second: Failure worship. This is where you

disregard the fact that projects (like life) have variations in the path from inception to completion. Failure worshippers see these variations as unplanned events, and therefore as failures, since we didn't account for them, even when the variation produces positive results. When you look for failure, you will find it, but when you worship failure (and most of us do this because we have been programmed to do it) you will not only find failure, you will ignore success as well. Third: Success blindness—See Failure worship. When we reverse this behavior by replacing it with the celebration of incremental victories, success begets success, and ultimately teams find ways to continuously improve performance rather than setting up systems whose only goal is to avoid the pain of failure (Remember Step 6?). Celebrate incremental victories! Take credit for jobs well done, and do them even better next time.

How I Did It

I am a firm believer in hard and soft targets. So I set them realistically, every day. Once I had come to the realization that it took years to gain the weight and it is more than likely going to take years to lose it, I could move forward without the pressure of trying to drop forty pounds before my next high school reunion which, by the way, is in two weeks. Once I was able to set the overall goals that I wanted to achieve over the course of the first year, the rest was easy. Each month had a hard target which was non-negotiable and a soft target which was just icing on the cake. Each week also provided more opportunities for attainable hard and soft targets which I posted internally and on my Facebook page. And trust me, when I missed it, I heard about it; and it was great as it served as a catalyst for improvement. After a while, I was celebrating every day, marking the failures in light of the victories and not the other way around. Start off with what you can do, even if it's only five push-ups once a day as a hard target, with a soft target of twice a day coupled with a half-mile walk. Knock that out and build on it. Like my Facebook page at facebook.com/pages/100-Small-Steps/621191304580263 and post your victories so we can share them together!

Be Held Accountable

*"The ultimate measure of a man is not
where he stands in moments of comfort
and convenience, but where he stands at
times of challenge and controversy."*
—**Martin Luther King Jr.**

What the Experts Say

Accountability is defined as an obligation or willingness
to accept responsibility or to account for one's actions.
Drs. Paul Gillard and Rachel Radwinsky are two of the
principles at Transformation Associates, Inc., a consulting,
technology, and training firm in Lebanon, New Jersey.
Their work deals with enterprise and departmental
transformations for some of the most recognizable brands
in the world. They take accountability even further and say
that without three key factors accountability *cannot* exist:

(1) Clear established goals that are relevant, realistic, and reportable; (2) Adequate resources and authority; and (3) having predetermined outcomes for both success and failure that are established, documented, and communicated. Accountability isn't simply a means by which we apply consequences to our failed actions, but a vehicle we can use to set ourselves up for continued success.

How I Did It

Once I got over the shame and "punish yourself" phases, I told everyone I knew about my weight loss goals and found ways to measure and track successes and failures in relation to the goals I set. Social media also played a huge role in my need to be held accountable for my actions and journey. My friends kept me honest and, most importantly, they kept me from doing stupid things like wanting to try steroids or going on some crazy crash diet. In essence I had a whole team of individuals cheering me on when I won and, when I fell flat, putting their arms around me and reminding me that according to my goals we were running a marathon, not a sprint, which encouraged me to take the next hill that much quicker. I believe the reason I was willing to accept my friends and loved ones holding my feet to the fire was because it didn't look, sound or feel like the typical judgment and shame that we often mistake for holding someone "accountable." They began from the position that I wanted to be successful as opposed to just validating their negative preconceived notions about my quest when I failed. Don't get me wrong: with accountability comes pressure and anxiety, but it's the good kind. The purposeful kind! Trust me when I tell you, it makes all the difference in the world.

Step 16 Questions

Feet to the Fire

"Goals give purpose. Purpose gives faith.
Faith gives courage. Courage gives enthusiasm.
Enthusiasm gives energy. Energy gives life.
Life lifts you over the bar."
—Bob Richards

1. Who am I accountable to today?
2. Who do I actually trust to hold my feet to the fire?
3. Does their version of "accountability" remind me of feeling judged or shamed?

Visualize the End Result

What the Experts Say

In a study published in *Psychology and Health*, McGill University's Dr. Bärbel Knäuper and her students asked 177 students at the new residence hall to set themselves the goal of consuming more fruit for a period of seven days.[1] The wonderful thing about this particular study is that all of the students actually did consume more fruit, but those who were instructed to make a plan, write it down, and then visualize themselves successfully implementing the plan, consumed twice as much fruit as those who simply set out to eat more fruit without doing so. This study reinforces what sports psychologists and elite athletes have known for years. When you create a mental picture using visualization, your subconscious mind records it as an actual event. This "false" memory actually helps to build confidence, crystallizes your vision and focus, and "greases the tracks," so to speak, so that you move more intuitively in positive ways to achieve your goals.

How I Did It

I started with meditation and learned how to kill two birds with one stone. If you remember back in Step 11, the focal point of my meditation was not just to create harmony between body and mind, but to actually "see" that harmony in action. Without even knowing it, I was creating in my subconscious eye "memories" that were to me real, tangible, pleasurable, and confidence-building. As those visualizations (eating healthier, feeling good about my healthy choices, etc.) manifested themselves in my actions and lower pants sizes, the difference between mere visualization and what was actually happening became blurred. That's when I knew it was working. That's when my journey turned the corner.

Step 17 Questions

What Does That Look Like?

*"Extraordinary people visualize not what
is possible or probable, but rather what
is impossible, and by visualizing the
impossible, they begin to see it as possible."*
—Cherie Carter-Scott

1. What does the new healthier me look like?
2. How does the new healthier me act?
3. How does the new healthier me think about food as fuel?

Take Your Credit Card Out of Your Wallet

"Shopping baskets have a larger proportion of food items rated as impulsive and unhealthy when shoppers use credit or debit cards to pay for the purchases."
—Journal of Consumer Research

What the Experts Say

In October 2010 three researchers from Cornel University, State University of New York, Binghamton, and State University of New York, Buffalo, published a study in the *Journal of Consumer Research* in which they posited that credit card purchases actually increase unhealthy food purchases.[1] They summarized the study in this way:

Some food items that are commonly considered unhealthy also tend to elicit impulsive responses. The pain of paying in cash can curb impulsive urges to purchase such unhealthy food products. Credit card payments, in contrast, are relatively painless and weaken impulse control. Consequently, consumers are more likely to buy unhealthy food products when they pay by credit card than when they pay in cash. Results from four studies support these hypotheses. Analysis of actual shopping behavior of 1,000 households over a period of 6 months revealed that shopping baskets have a larger proportion of food items rated as impulsive and unhealthy when shoppers use credit or debit cards to pay for the purchases.

How I Did It

I've always believed that one of the worst things that happened to us was the loosening of the minimum credit-card purchase amounts. Just ten years ago, a responsible individual would never have thought of putting a $6 cup of coffee on her credit card. But the card companies love the volume of transactions due to our collective irresponsibility. You know what the industry calls someone that never carries a balance on her card? A deadbeat. Yep, be responsible, pay on time, build a good credit rating, and what will they do? They'll increase your spending limit so they can tempt you into irresponsible behavior, which includes throwing that extra bag of doughnuts, a bottle of soda, and a bag of chips right into the shopping cart. Now, my financial situation isn't the best, so it really wasn't hard for me, but I put myself on cash rations. When I ran out of money for fuel (food, that is), I was in trouble. It only took a couple of times running out of money on Thursday before I stopped dipping into the fuel fund for indulgences. I did not deprive myself of fuel, but since I had to pay cash for it, and cash was a limited resource, I made much better choices about my fuel. I purchased the items that gave me the biggest nutritional bang for my dollar and went further (Junk-food packaging is notoriously small and mostly air). What did I do with the card, you ask? I froze it in a bowl of water.

Keep It Simple

"Muscles don't grow in the gym."
—**"Two-Meal" Mike O'Donnell**

What the Experts Say

"Two-Meal" Mike O'Donnell has a blog entitled The IF Life, where he espouses the simple two-meal lifestyle. Mike likes to keep everything simple. Diet and nutrition, exercise and tracking are all done for maximum efficiency and sanity control. "I see it in every gym, people giving 110 percent doing some of the craziest things. People spending hours and hours in there daily for 7x a week, yet they look the same month after month. Clients spending $1000/ month on private training yet their trainer has them doing stuff that is not even related to what their goals are. What is going on?" Keep it simple.

- Don't worry about how many calories you're burning during workouts. Diet and nutrition are 85 percent of your results.
- Muscles don't grow in the gym. Keep your workouts to thirty minutes, then go home and get some rest.
- Have a simple workout plan and keep rest periods short.
- You don't need a gym to have a good workout.

How I Did It

I refused to go to the gym to show everyone my obesity, so I had to learn how to do what I could do at home. I started with stair push-ups and step-ups. I added jumping jacks, deep knee-bends, and sit-ups. Then I got my hands on a copy of *Convict Conditioning* by Paul "Coach" Wade and learned about burpees and all sorts of bad-ass bodyweight conditioning exercises and techniques like table pull-ups, chair dips, doorway chest-flies, and the dreaded one-legged squat (which, by the way, this fat guy still cannot do!). Guess what? You can work up a sweat, lose weight, and get in better shape without dragging yourself to a gym. So there! No more excuses for you!

Step 19 Questions

What's the Plan?

"It takes as much energy to wish as it does to plan."
—Eleanor Roosevelt

What can I start doing today to be more active:

1. At home

2. At work

3. At play

It's Gonna Hurt— Get Over It!

"Pain is weakness leaving the body"
—**Lt. General Lewis B. "Chesty" Puller, USMC**

What the Experts Say

"Pain is weakness leaving the body"
—**Lt. General Lewis B. "Chesty" Puller, USMC, (c. 1955)**

How I Did It

At first I cried, a lot, and then my six-year old daughter Michaela (the Cheesy Poofs queen) asked me one day what was making me so upset all the time. I told her how I had allowed myself to get so fat and out of shape, and how hard it was to do just these simple exercises that left my back, legs, and neck hurting so badly. My daughter has a great and ever-present smile, but she wasn't smiling and I could see that she was thinking hard. She then put her hand on my shoulder and said, "Remember when I kept falling off my bike, Daddy, and skinning my knees?" I said, "Yes, baby girl, I do. You would cry and cry and I would hold your hand until you felt better." She then asked me, "Do you remember what you told me about the next time? You said the next time I wouldn't cry so much, because I already knew it was going to hurt. I already know what it feels like, so it won't be a surprise and after a while it wouldn't even hurt anymore. I could take chances and fall all I wanted after that. You already know it's gonna hurt. Right, Daddy?" With tears in my eyes I looked at this wise and wondrous young six-year old and said simply, "You're right, baby, I do. Thank you for reminding me." This reminds me of Psalm 8:2: "You have taught children and infants to tell of your strength, silencing your enemies and all who oppose you."

Have a Cheat Day Every Week

"Honey buns are overrated!"
—Temple

What the Experts Say

The experts over at Fitday.com sum it up this way. "Many dieters think that having a *cheat day* [emphasis in the original] amounts to failure, so they either struggle to avoid the temptation altogether or they feel incredibly guilty after they cheat on their diet and engage in some behaviors that are more damaging to their diet in the long run. While it's true that taking time off from your diet can cause some problems, there are some very important reasons to approach "cheating" that can aid in your physical and mental health." The "Cheat Day" philosophy they espouse is simple:

- Understand the cheat day. This is not a license to spend an entire day eating like a teenager. Choose one meal and treat yourself to something banned from your diet.
- Plan for your cheat day. If you have a cheat day to look forward to, you will be less likely to be in danger of binge eating.
- Having a cheat day increases your motivation to stick to the healthy lifestyle you have chosen for yourself and makes you less susceptible to ego depletion.

How I Did It

In this area I didn't become more disciplined until later in the journey, and I was seriously going to hurt someone if I didn't get my cheesy-poof or honey-bun fix. I had spent several months trying to avoid all the foods that were bad for me, but in the course of trying to be healthy I was engaged in the unhealthy and counterproductive activity of spending ninety percent of my waking hours thinking about and craving what I was depriving myself of. Talk about ego depletion! At the end of the day I was exhausted and unmotivated. Once I incorporated a cheat day into my weekly regimen, slowly but surely the cravings went away. I started out taking the entire day to eat whatever I wanted, but the healthier I got, the less appealing it became and finally I was cheating "the right way," which for me was one special meal where I ate what I wanted in moderation. I knew I had turned the corner when I wrote in my journal: "5:15 pm, really craving a honey bun…. 5:45 pm: honey buns are overrated!" I haven't had one since, and that was more than a year ago.

Step 21 Questions

Cheater! Cheater!

Does knowing that it's normal and ok to have a cheat day every week help you feel better about the journey now?

If so, why?

Television Is Not Your Weight-Loss Friend

"Too much time sitting, at work or at home, increases the risk of becoming obese, and may also increase the risk of chronic diseases and early death."
—**Harvard School of Public Health**

What the Experts Say

Americans spend, on average, approximately five hours per day watching television,[1] but this isn't the full picture of our total "screen time" which is contributing to our more sedentary lifestyle. Most of us work desk jobs, watch television, play video games, drive to and from work, and use tablet PC's as part of our recreational downtime (and this is after using a computer for eight hours a day). Evidence is emerging that too much time sitting, whether at work or at home, increases the risk of becoming obese and may also contribute to chronic disease and early death. What is unclear is whether the act of sitting itself is the culprit or whether sitting is just a marker of other unhealthy aspects of our modern lifestyle (vis-à-vis television watching or other screen time) that is primarily responsible for the trends. It is possible, however, that other types of sedentary lifestyles and behaviors promote overeating in different ways: reading e-mail and taking work home may increase stress (remember Step 10?) which can lead to overeating, while listening to music may distract you from even noticing how much you are eating even when you're not really hungry. Matt Denos, PhD is a biologist and writer interested in obesity treatment research and issues related to nutrition, weight-loss, and medical diet programs. He writes that there are at least five ways that just watching TV can make you fat:

- The powerful brainwashing effects of food advertising
- Increased calorie consumption
- Unhealthy eating
- A slower metabolic rate
- The tendency to eat more at succeeding meals

How I Did It

I am a huge movie buff and can sit on a couch watching movies all day and well into the night. Whenever I didn't have any money, or had nothing planned with the kids, it was big bowls of popcorn and either *The Lord of the Rings* or *Harry Potter* movie marathons. We did it all wrong and I was the culprit, teaching my children the terrible habits of mindless eating while lowering their resting metabolic rates and setting them up for possible chronic disease or early death. I love my children with my heart and soul, but after reading articles on screen time I realized I was contributing to the problem in a big way and damaging the health of people whom I loved. Some dad, huh? My wife Rebecca had always sought to restrict screen time to a couple of hours a day and I thought that was extreme. Now I was the one restricting screen time and trying to find low-cost ways to get us out of the house, even in the winter. Winter was the hard part. I'm from Texas and I never got over moving to Chicago right before the blizzard of 1979. So, needless to say, Old Man Winter and I don't exactly see eye-to-eye. The kids didn't seem to like him either. It usually took them thirty minutes or less to come running back into the house. So we decided to get everyone good winter clothing so that we could all stay active even when it was cold outside. The difference was night and day. It's amazing how warm you can be when you buy for function over looks. We were outside for hours and no one was running around holding their hands in agonizing pain like we did when we were kids. We were still together laughing, playing, being active, and not allowing the couch to drive us all into an early grave. I even went hunting for the first time since my dad took me when we were in Texas. I knew we were finally doing it right when someone asked me about a popular TV show and I had no idea what he was talking about.

Dress Well All the Time

*"If you can't see it, then you aren't
likely to be motivated to change it."*
—Tammy Strome

What the Experts Say

Tammy Strome, owner of Tammy Strome Fitness and co-
founder of Cre8ion Fitness & Wellness, Inc. really puts the
spotlight on this topic. You're hiding in your fat clothes.
"If you can't see it, then you aren't likely to be motivated
to change it." If you remember, in Step 4 I had stopped
acknowledging the fact that I was obese and just bought
bigger clothes, which is just counterproductive. Tammy,
who is the mother of two (though you would never know
it just by looking at her), gives the following advice.
First, take those clothes off at home and take an honest
inventory. Look at your body and acknowledge it as it is

at this moment. It will hurt, but that hurt is needed for lasting change. Be kind to yourself and don't allow your "fat goggles" to cloud your vision. And secondly, if you don't have any clothes that fit properly now, go out and buy some that are flattering to your body type as it is today. Men, shine your shoes, buy a pocket square, and trim those stray hairs. Ladies, get your hair and nails done, and do something new with your makeup. Feeling good at all stages gives you the incentive and motivation to stick to your "get fit" plans. The compliments that will come don't hurt either.

How I Did It

I bought four really nice shirts at a Brooks Brothers store at the Dolphin Mall in Miami and they did not fit me. They sat in my closet for three years. When I finally got serious about making the transformation, I made a monthly ritual of trying each one on and marking how far I had to go in order to wear one without looking like an overstuffed sausage. In a sense they acted as another physical form of my progress, so I called them my "progress shirts." In the meantime, I went out and bought clothes that fit a little tighter than I was comfortable with and gave my size 60 pants and 4xl, 5xl, and 6xl shirts to Goodwill. As those clothes got "bigger" on me, I would swap them out with smaller clothes from Goodwill. I'm not at all ashamed to say I shopped there for my clothes. Losing weight is hard on your wardrobe budget, especially if, like me, you have almost two-hundred pounds to lose. I could go through a couple of pants sizes every ninety days and I refused to keep my "fat clothes" around for fear that I would get complacent and just put them back on if I gained a few pounds. The best thing that happened was that a bunch of us started losing weight together and started swapping clothes. As we got smaller we would give or sell our bigger clothes to someone in the group that fit them. If no one could fit them, we went right back to Goodwill. I think I made out like a bandit. The guy whose size I finally reached was in the mortgage business. Needless to say, he dressed very well; now I do, too.

Make Routines, Like Brushing Your Teeth after Meals

"There is no such thing as continuous improvement without continuous innovation."
—Don Galer

What the Experts Say

At Lifescript.com Dr. James Beckerman writes a Daily Diet Tip column and suggests that brushing your teeth after meals using a minty toothpaste can actually help facilitate weight loss by making sweet desserts and snacks less appealing. Everyone knows you just don't drink OJ after brushing your teeth (unless you want to know first-hand what an earwax-and-booger jelly bean tastes like). This is due to an ingredient in toothpaste (sodium lauryl sulfate) which is used to create that sudsy sensation and make your mouth feel clean. It also has the effect of turning off your tongue's sweet receptors and putting the bitter receptors on steroids. Voila! Willpower in a tube. Do this right after your meal which is when you are most likely to crave sweet desserts or snacks. This activity has the power to do two things. First, it builds the routine that tells your mind and body, "I am done eating; stop producing ghrelin" (referenced in Step 2). And secondly, it provides a physical barrier to eating that is pretty tough to overcome, unless of course you like earwax-and-booger-flavored snacks and desserts.

How I Did It

I wish I had known about the toothpaste deal earlier in my journey, but it was so effective that I had to share it! The routines that I developed for myself were: (1) I always ate at the table. When I left the table, I was finished. I never sat at the table for more than twenty minutes and I never went back. This included all meals. If I wasn't at a table, I wasn't eating. (2) I had a salad before each meal and a large glass of water. If I was still hungry, I had another salad and glass of water. (3) I slowed down and chewed my food at least twenty times. This aids in digestion and turns off the production of ghrelin, and finally: (4) I found out about brushing my teeth. Trust me when I tell you: honey buns and Colgate don't mix.

Never, Ever Go Grocery Shopping Hungry

"Plan your meals for the week BEFORE you shop."
—Cynthia Jeffcoat

What the Experts Say

The National Institutes of Health has this to say on the subject. Shop smart by planning ahead and asking yourself these two key questions[1]: (1) When and where will you be eating over the next week? (2) How much time will you have to cook? Once you have established this, then you should plan your meals for the week *before* you shop. Make a shopping list from your meal plan and take it with you, then promise yourself that you will not purchase items not on the list. Never go grocery shopping when you're hungry. You will make better choices if you shop after you have had a healthy meal or snack. Avoid buying in bulk and shopping in warehouse-type stores. Buying in quantity and getting a good deal can lead to over eating. If you do buy in larger quantities, divide every item into smaller sizes and store what you are not going to use immediately.

How I Did It

I avoided convenience stores and gas stations like the plague, and when I couldn't use the pay-at-the-pump option I made sure that I was only going to gas stations where I knew they had a bowl of fruit on the counter. This took an enormous amount of pre-thought and planning which is where my lessons on being "present" paid off for me. If I got caught in a store hungry, I immediately started drinking water, or if I didn't have my water I picked up some, paid for it, and left. After drinking the water, if I was still hungry I had a protein shake (I kept a tub in the car, another in my office, and another at home) and then went shopping. As I said, it takes a tremendous amount of effort, and I'm not perfect at it, but once you make it part of your daily routine it gets easier. And the best part about it is that when you've learned how to refuel the body properly, you won't be as hungry anyway and these episodes will be few and far between.

Learn to Love Yourself

*"Resentment is one burden that is incompatible
with your success. Always be the first to forgive
and forgive yourself first always."*
—Dan Zadra

What the Experts Say

Dr. Lissa Rankin, founder of the Owning Pink Center, writes a column for *Psychology Today* called Owning Pink. In her July 2010 post she posited that "…you will never achieve and maintain a healthy weight until you learn to love yourself, fat and all. If your weight loss is fueled by negative mind chatter and self-hatred, weight loss becomes punishment."[1] She then goes on to say that you must practice loving acceptance of the divine radiant being that you are. You must come to the realization that the spiritual aspect of our existence is perfect, whole, and weightless, regardless of what the world sees on the outside. "As long as you try to punish yourself into losing weight, even if you wind up 100 pounds skinnier, you will still hate yourself." When you love yourself, weight loss is sustainable. "Believe in yourself. Love Yourself. Be whole. You know you already are."

How I Did It

I started out heavy on the punishment side. If I was in a committed relationship with myself I would have been guilty of domestic violence, for sure. I berated myself and held myself accountable for every moment of weakness. Somewhere along the line someone asked me why I thought I was so much better and stronger than the rest of the planet. I was holding myself to an impossible standard of performance and willpower. During one of my counseling sessions I took a test and one of the inventory questions was "Do you like yourself?" You're supposed to answer the question with the first answer that pops into your head. The problem was I didn't have an answer. I hadn't really thought about it, but I was aware enough to realize that one of my coping mechanisms was that having no answer to a tough question was just my way of saying No. That is when I realized I had a serious issue to deal with. I started by making a list of the things I liked about myself, and then a list of the things I didn't like, and a pattern emerged. The things I liked about myself were real and substantive (loving, honest, intelligent, loyal, etc). The things I didn't like were based on shallow, worldly wants and desires (broke, fat, crappy car, etc.). I had become "that guy." You've seen him, the "one-up" king, so busy trying to keep up with the Joneses that he's lost who he is along the way. I had to make peace with who I really wanted to be as a person and start loving that guy, and what's more, allowing those who cared for me to love me too. It sounds easy, but it wasn't. Divorce is never easy, but in the end Mr. One Up, my false self, got screwed. He got to keep all the disappointment and I, the real me, got real relationships based on the love of a guy that in the end turned out not to be so bad after all. Now that's winning!

Step 26 Questions

Me, Myself, and I

1. What do you like about yourself?
2. What do you dislike?
3. Are you being fair to yourself?

Don't Watch the Food

"In 2010 food-makers spent $11.3B to sell food.
The USDA spent $268M to educate."
—**Journal of the**
American Dietetic Association

What the Experts Say

In June 2010 *Time* magazine published an article entitled "What if you ate only what was advertised on TV?" The article was based on research published in the *Journal of the American Dietetic Association* which suggests that TV ads for food may be skewing our decisions in powerful ways. To better understand how unhealthy a TV-guided diet would be, researchers studied food commercials that appeared during eighty-four hours of prime-time programming and twelve hours of Saturday morning cartoons broadcast over the major U.S. Networks.[1]

Their findings are based on a two-thousand calorie per day diet containing only foods that were advertised and are as follows:

- Exceeds the recommended daily amount of fat by 20 times.
- Contains 25 times the recommended daily intake of sugar.
- Provides less than half the recommended daily intake of fruit, vegetables, and dairy.
- In the year the study took place, food-makers spent $11.3 billion to sell, but the United States Department of Agriculture (USDA) spent only $268 million to educate.

How do you defend yourself and your family? Don't watch the food.

How I Did It

We don't watch TV all that much, and even when we do watch TV we always mute the commercials. And not just the food commercials—all commercials. One of my favorite shows was about a guy who went around the country taking on the most outrageous food challenges. He started off looking very fit, ballooned up, then went back to looking fit. One day it dawned on me that I was watching this man kill himself, literally! So I stopped watching that show and all food shows, cold turkey. And I remember writing in my notes that it seems like I'm not fighting the cravings as much. Is that happening because I stopped watching the food?

Network With and Befriend Fit People

"We are highly influenced by the people closest to us. Surrounding yourself with healthy people tends to make you healthy by association."
—Tony Schober

What the Experts Say

Tony Schober, a health and fitness blogger and the founder of CoachCalorie.com, tells us that if you look at the healthy people in the world you would begin to notice patterns of choice and behaviors that many of them would have in common. So, in a variation on a theme, he compiled the "10 Habits of Exceptionally Healthy People." Habit 4 reads that "They surround themselves with other healthy people." Schober continues, "We are highly influenced by the people closest to us. Surrounding yourself with healthy people tends to make you healthy by association. Not only are you motivated and inspired by your healthy friends, but there's also a sense of social pressure to be healthy yourself when you're around them."

How I Did It

Remember Step 14? That step was all about inviting positive reinforcement into your life and removing toxic people. Now this step is about replacing those "toxic influencers" with people who are already living the lifestyle you want to live. This part is not easy if you're an introvert, but I'm not one, so I went up to fit people at the gym, at work, whenever and wherever there was an opportunity, and just told them my goals. You would be surprised at how willing people are to engage with you when you earn their trust by proving that you're committed. For a lot of healthy people, being healthy is a passion and it is one that they will share pretty freely. It's called being a catalyst and once you've been around them long enough you will become one too. It's a cheesy Star Wars line, but ultimately student becomes master and the cycle starts again.

Step 28 Question

A Little Help from My Friends

Are my friends mostly fit or could they be considered overweight?

Get Active Socially

"We are highly influenced by the people closest to us. Surrounding yourself with healthy people tends to make you healthy by association."
—Tony Schober

What the Experts Say

Chrissy Wallace of CrossFit Duval helped me to understand this better than anyone else who wrote on the topic. In her words, "Suffering together breeds companionship." It creates a sense of community and relatability that you can't build working out or running on your own. Moreover it creates accountability through friendly competition. Who wants to be the individual always at the bottom of the standings, finishing last, not accomplishing her or his goals week after week, especially when there are your fellow warriors cheering you on and carrying you the last few feet? Wallace writes, "The mind will quit hundreds of times before the body will, but no one wants to be the one that lets their partner down!"

How I Did It

I am blessed to have great friends who were supportive and eager to join me in my journey, and to live in St. Croix County, Wisconsin, where the St. Croix River flows clean and free. The St. Croix is the natural border between far western Wisconsin and far eastern Minnesota. It is a stunningly beautiful place to be and it's loaded with walking and biking trails, swimming, boating, beach volleyball, and other activities. I coordinated a Saturday morning bike ride from the marina in Hudson, Wisconsin, to the marina in Afton, Minnesota. Trust me when I tell you that this was no ride in the park. I had no idea that it was possible to go uphill both ways on a trip, but this ride certainly felt like it. The first hurdle was the Interstate 94 bridge and it just got better from there. Sixteen miles roundtrip of quad-and-glute busting and humping that kept each of us honest, and challenging each other to go faster, rest less, and get there first. You can't beat fellowship like that, especially when you realize that you're not only helping each other, but helping each other's families live healthy and more productive lives.

Step 29 Questions

Ready, Set, Go!

How am I currently active with my:

1. Family
2. Friends
3. Co-workers
4. Community

Read Into It!

What the Experts Say

At the signing of the Intermediate-Range Nuclear Forces Treaty, on December 8, 1987, Ronald Reagan said, "Trust, but verify." Suzanne Massie, the daughter of a Swiss diplomat and author of *Land of the Firebird: The Beauty of Old Russia*, taught Reagan this phrase after he read her book and invited her to the White House. Afterwards, she became sort-of a back-door messenger between Reagan and Russian General Secretary Mikhail Gorbachev towards the end of the Cold War. The phrase, in essence, states this: though the source of your information may be credible and reliable, a prudent individual will perform additional research to verify that the information is accurate and trustworthy. In other words, don't just read this book and take my word for it. Read into it and see if you can find the flaws.

How I Did It

As you can see here, I wrote things down that worked for me and then set about proving to myself that there was scientific evidence and the personal experiences of other successful weight-loss journeys that matched my own. I didn't even take my own word for it. Be ever skeptical of the get-skinny-quick crowds and homemade remedies that may just be on-offs that work in the short term but not for a lifetime. Strive to be healthy and whole, not just give the appearance of such.

Keep a Journal

"Writing, expressing can heal us. It can focus, support, and enhance our lives and well-being. Whether we laugh or we cry, whether through sorrow or joy, we can understand more about ourselves, and each other, through keeping a journal."
—Doreene Clement

What the Experts Say

The people over at the Ririan Project, RirianProject.com, came up with the ten best reasons I never had for keeping a journal. I love it when what I am doing by instinct is validated in the real world and through my own results. See how many correlations with the Steps so far you can find here. It gave me goose bumps! So without further ado, here goes. You keep a journal to:

- Improve your health
- Reduce stress
- Build stronger relationships
- Gain better organizational skills
- Achieve better focus
- Better problem solving
- Know yourself better
- Foster personal growth
- Enhance intuition and creativity
- Capture your story

How I Did It

You're reading it, kid! But I do have some tips (once again validated by the Ririan Project people!) for how to get started, stay motivated and keep yourself on track:

- Write every day at the same time, if you can. Find a place where you will not be disturbed and just get after it.
- Write for at least ten minutes, even if it's only gibberish at first. Trust me, your voice will come, and when it does you will find that ten minutes isn't enough time.
- No one is here to critique your spelling or grammar (which, by the way, is quite liberating) and if they do, you have my permission to tell 'em to kiss where the sun don't shine (also liberating and quite satisfying). The important thing is to keep writing.

- It's your journal, so say what you want. Don't spend any time trying to censor yourself. Now, if you find your writing turning dark, then clearly you have skipped Step 7. Go back to Step 7 and see it through!

Step 31 Question

Pens and Swords

How much writing have you done just answering the questions in this book? (You see what I just did there, don't cha?)

Book That Vacation

"Ya coo tacha, cap u nu nee sa"
—Jabba the Hutt

This is all about creating some calendar pressure for yourself. If you remember back in Step 23, I bought the shirts. The money was gone and I either had to get the work done to wear the shirts or they would collect dust, or be given away. Now the reason it took so long was due to the fact that I had a successful consulting business so there was no pressure to get into those shirts. Unfortunately (or fortunately, depending on how you look at it), for me the business went south and I couldn't just go down to the store whenever I needed a new shirt anymore. That was the catalyst for me. I needed new clothes. At the same time, my girls wanted to go to the Dells, a waterparks vacation site in Wisconsin. So let's back up. When my beloved Michaela was born I used to love to hold her close to me as often as I could, since I traveled so much. One day I was holding her on the coach without a shirt on and my son Noah walked up to me and said in his best gravelly voice, "Hu Hu Hu Hu, Ya coo tacha, cap u nu nee sa," and then proceeded to die laughing. We're big Star Wars geeks so I knew exactly what he was talking about. The little bastard was saying that I looked like Jabba the Hutt sitting there with little Michaela on the couch! Fast forward a couple of years and I was mortified at the thought of being seen out there like that. We booked the vacation, but I was determined to lose some weight before it happened. It was then that I realized I had been depriving my family of quality vacation time because I was ashamed of how I looked. I didn't want to look like the typical Wisconsinite tipping the scales at almost four-hundred pounds so I got busy making the changes necessary to feel a little better about myself. I didn't go on a crash diet but I had very specific goals about how much I wanted to lose by the time we went. Guess what? I didn't make the goal, but I was close, and we had a great time. Book that vacation even if it is just for yourself. Call it part of your Step 15 regimen.

Be a Catalyst

"There ain't no rules around here.
We're trying to accomplish something!"
—Thomas Edison

What the Experts Say

Sherri, over at SereneJourney.com, says this about change, "You are more likely to be accepting of change when you are the creator and more likely to oppose it when it is forced upon you." If that isn't right out of Step 1, then nothing is! Nothing was more motivating for me than telling my story and then seeing the change happen in other people and watching them "infect" the next person. A catalyst is defined here as someone that causes something to happen, and when we look at these people they share four key traits:

- They take the initiative to make things happen.
- They positively promote new directions and ideas.
- They make change manageable.
- They are agile in their actions and in how they think.

Looking at this list, can you say that you have the potential to be your own catalyst? If not, what do you need to do in order to become one? If the first step is to know why you're doing it, then, really, the second is learning how to be a catalyst or change agent, initially in your own life and then in the lives of others.

How I Did It

I did this without even knowing it, to be honest with you. If you remember, back in Step 16 I was telling everyone I knew about my weight-loss goals so that they could hold me accountable. What I did not realize at the time was that I was taking the initiative to make that happen in their lives as well. And as they saw me talking the talk and then walking the walk, they joined in. We all positively promoted the idea that we needed to be healthy enough to enjoy our vices and we made the change manageable by holding each other to setting and achieving realistic goals that did not put our overall health in danger (that is, no crash diets, steroids, general stupidity). And none of this could have happened if we were not agile in our actions and thinking. Thanks, Sherri, for putting the icing on this part of my journey cake.

You Gotta Eat Right

For me, this is one of the most difficult subjects to deal with because of the programming that I had been subjected to all of my life. Everything was about food: from the earliest guilt from my mom about starving kids in Africa, and why we needed to clean our plates, to the whole sports bar you-gotta-be-chuggin'-a-beer-and-eatin'-something-fried in order to be one of the cool kids peer pressure. From a young age we are programmed unwittingly by our parents and nefariously by big food companies vying for our brand loyalty to closely associate our well-being with the copious and utterly unnecessary over-consumption of food, and mainly carbohydrates. Food is precious to us and occupies an elevated place of worship in our social constructs so be aware that the process of learning how to undo the damage and get on the right path will be difficult and filled with false starts. Part of this nefarious and unwitting training started with the United States Department of Agriculture's introduction of what would eventually become the food pyramid as we know it today. The pyramid was initially developed in 1941 when Franklin Delano Roosevelt prompted a National Nutrition Conference. The output of this conference was, for the first time, the USDA recommended daily allowances for American's to follow. It also specified caloric intake and nutritional guidelines essential for healthy living. During the second year of our involvement in World War II (1943), the USDA introduced the "Basic 7," a special modification of the nutritional guidelines to help people deal with the shortage of food. Because of its complexity, the "Basic 7" was later revised to the "Basic 4" and was taught as gospel until the 1970's when a fifth category was added. In order to deal with the rise in chronic diseases (i.e., strokes and heart disease), fats, sweets, and alcoholic beverages were added as "unhealthy foods to be consumed in moderation," and thus the food pyramid was complete. A diet modified for a people at war, suffering from a shortage of food, who needed lots of breads and grains to feel full, while mostly working in manufacturing and agrarian jobs, is what we, the office-working, couch-lounging, carb-craving masses of today have been swearing by and dying from ever since.

Notes

Foreword

1. A 2012 study in *The American Journal of Preventive Medicine* concluded that by 2030, 42 percent of adults will be obese. http://www.cdc.gov/chronicdisease/overview/index.htm#ref9

Step 1

1. *Archives of General Psychiatry* 67 (March 2010): 220-29, www.medscape.com/viewarticle/718012.
2. www.cdc.gov/brfss/publications/ssummaries.htm. Get America Fit Foundation, www.getamericafit.org/statistics-obesity-in-america.html.

Step 2

1. *Health Psychology* 4 (July 30, 2011): 424-29; Discussion 430-31, www.ncbi.nlm.nih/gov/pubmed/21574706.
2. Ibid.

Step 3

1. W. F. Kellogg Foundation, cited in Jill Richardson, "Behind the Shady World of Marketing Junk Food to Children," AlterNet (March 22, 2010): 2, www.alternet.org/story/146093/behind_the_shady_world_of_marketing_junk_food_to_children.

Step 7

1. Playing the dozens is a pursuit in which a person attempts to outwit another by deriding him or her with a greater and more prodigious succession of insults.

2. This is an example of a snap: "Man, you so dumb. Somebody said it was chilly outside so you went and got a bowl."

3. www.depressionperception.com/depression/depression_facts_and_statistics.asp.

4. Ibid.

Step 8

1. James Neel (1962), cited in Christopher W. Kuzawa, "Beyond Feast-Famine: Brain Evolution, Human Life History, and the Metabolic Syndrome," http://groups.anthropology.northwestern.edu/lhbr/kuzawa_web_files/pdfs/Kuzawa%20-%20feast%20famine%20chapter.pdf.

2. Piggly Wiggly is a supermarket chain operating in the Midwest and Southern regions of the United States, founded in Memphis, Tennessee, in 1916.

Step 9

1. John Tierney, "Do You Suffer From Decision Fatigue?" *New York Times* (August 17, 2011), http://www.nytimes.com/2011/08/21/magazine/do-you-suffer-from-decision-fatigue.html?pagewanted=1&r=3.
2. A beat down is the act of receiving a serious beating at the hands of a person or group of persons

Step 10

1. *American Journal of Physiology – Regulatory, Integrative and Comparative Physiology*, 299, no. R813-R822 (September 1, 2010), cited in "Link Between Everyday Stress and Obesity Strengthened With Study Using an Animal Model," *Science Daily* (September 2, 2010), http://www.sciencedaily.com/releases/2010/09/100901145250.htm.

Step 11

1. Vedanta is the chief Hindu philosophy dealing mainly with the Upanishadic doctrine of the identity of Brahman and Atman that reached its highest development c. 800 CE through the philosopher Shankara.

Step 12

1. Steven A. Burd, "How Safeway Is Cutting Health-Care Costs," *Wall Street Journal* (updated

June 12, 2009), http://online.wsj.com/article/
SB124476804026308603.html.

Step 13
1. "Emotional Eating and Weight Loss," http://www.
webmd.com/diet/emotional-eating.

Step 17
1. Bärbel Knäuper et al., "Fruitful Plans: Adding
Targeted Mental Imagery to Implementation
Intentions Increases Fruit Consumption," *Psychology
and Health* 26, no. 5 (2011), http://www.tandfonline.
com/doi/abs/10.1080/08870441003703218
(February 18, 2011).

Step 18
1. Manoj Thomas, Kalpesh Kaushik Desai, and
Satheeshkumar Seenivasan, "How Credit Card
Payments Increase Unhealthy Food Purchases:
Visceral Regulation of Vices," *Journal of
Consumer Research* 38 (June 2011), http://
forum.johnson.cornell.edu/faculty/mthomas/
VisceralRegulationofVices.pdf (October 6, 2010).

Step 22
1. Harvard School of Public Health, "Television
Watching and 'Sit Time,'" http://www.hsph.harvard.
edu/obesity-prevention-source/obesity-causes/
television-and-sedentary-behavior-and-obesity/.

Step 25

1. National Institutes of Health, "Healthy Grocery Shopping," MedlinePlus, http://www.nlm.nih.gov/medlineplus/ency/patientinstructions/000336.htm (updated November 12, 2012).

Step 26

1. http://www.psychologytoday.com/blog/owning-pink/201007/how-lose-weight-love

Step 27

1. Alice Park, "What if You Ate Only What Was Advertised on TV?" *Time* (June 2, 2010), http://content.time.com/time/health/article/0,8599,1993220,00.html.

Glossary

agile project management. Agile management or agile project management is an iterative and incremental method of managing the design-and-build activities for engineering, information technology, and new-product or service-development projects in a highly flexible and interactive manner.

agrarian. Related to farming or the cultivation of land

Basic 4. The "Basic 4" food groups was a simplification of the "Basic 7" and categorized foods in this manner: fruits and vegetables, dairy, meat, and cereals.

Basic 7. The "Basic 7" food groups were introduced in 1943 and were as follows: minerals, water, fats, protein, carbohydrates, vitamins and fiber.

biometric screening. The measurement of physical characteristics, such as height, weight, body mass index, blood pressure, blood cholesterol, blood glucose (sugar), and aerobic fitness tests

body mass index (BMI). A measure of body fat that is the ratio of the weight of the body in kilograms to the square of its height in meters

calendar pressure. A deadline set by inviting people to a meeting for which you must provide the materials. By the way, you haven't created the materials yet.

calories. A unit of energy

carbohydrate. Any of a group of organic compounds that includes sugars, starches, celluloses, and gums and serves as a major energy source in the diet of animals. These compounds are produced by photosynthetic plants and contain only carbon, hydrogen, and oxygen.

chronic disease. A disease that is long lasting or recurrent

coping mechanisms. A behavioral tool that may be used by individuals to offset or overcome adversity, disadvantage, or disability. My coping mechanisms were maladaptive, that is, non-coping, and usually took place after a stressor had been introduced.

cortisol. See **hydrocortisone.**

decision fatigue. Refers to the deteriorating quality of decisions made by an individual after a long session of decision making.

Diagnostic and Statistical Manual of Mental Disorders. Better known as the DSM-IV. This manual categorizes psychiatric diagnosis and is published by the American Psychiatric Association and covers all mental health disorders for children and adults.

dysfunction. Abnormal or impaired functioning, especially of a bodily system or social group

ego depletion. Refers to the idea that self-control and willpower draw upon a limited pool of mental resources that can be used up over time.

enabler. One that enables another to achieve an end; especially one who enables another to persist in self-destructive behavior (i.e., substance abuse) by providing excuses or by making it possible to avoid the consequences of such behavior.

Gen Xer. Generation X is described as the generation born between 1965 and 1984.

ghrelin. A hormone produced in the body that stimulates appetite

glute. Short for Gluteus Maximus, the broad, thick, outermost muscle of the buttocks

hard target. A realistic, non-negotiable goal that must be met

holistic. Characterized by the treatment of the whole person, taking into account mental, physical, spiritual, and social factors, rather than just the physical alone

hydrocortisone. An adrenal-cortex hormone that is active in carbohydrate and protein metabolism. Also called cortisol.

insulin. A hormone produced in the pancreas that regulates the amount of glucose (a type of sugar) in the blood

insulin resistance. A condition where the cells of the body are less responsive to insulin and where glucose is less able to enter the cells remaining in the blood stream

Lean Six Sigma. Lean Six Sigma is a managerial concept combining Lean and Six

Sigma that results in the elimination of the seven kinds of wastes, or muda (classified as transportation, inventory, motion, waiting, overproduction, over-processing, and defects)

meta-analysis. Refers to a research strategy where, instead of conducting new research with participants, the researchers examine the results of several previous studies.

metabolic rate. Rate of metabolism; the amount of energy expended in a given period

morbidly obese. An adult with a Body Mass Index of 40 or greater is considered morbidly obese.

obese. An adult with a Body Mass Index of 30 or greater is considered obese.

overweight. According to the Centers for Disease Control, an adult with a Body Mass Index between 25 and 29.9 is considered overweight.

peptide. A compound consisting of two or more amino acids in which the carboxyl group of one acid is linked to the amino group of the other

screen time. The time spent in front of an electronic device. This includes television, video games, DVD movies, e-mail, instant messaging, non-school related computer usage. Pediatricians and child development experts now recommend children's screen time be limited to no more than two hours per day.

soft target. A goal that is more challenging than the hard target, but does not represent failure if not achieved.

toxic influencers. Any person or power that negatively influences your behavior

USDA. United States Department of Agriculture

3 1270 00761 7477

CPSIA information can be obtained at www.ICGtesting.com
Printed in the USA
BVOW05s1735231214

380619BV00004B/232/P

9 781630 471804